WE ARE THE SHIP
The Story of NEGRO LEAGUE BASEBALL

Words and Paintings by **KADIR NELSON**

Foreword by **Hank Aaron**

JUMP AT THE SUN HYPERION/*New York*

AN IMPRINT OF DISNEY BOOK GROUP

"He could squat down on his honkers
and throw you out."

— Crush Holloway, outfielder for the Indianapolis ABCs, on Biz Mackey

"Cool could turn out the light and be under the covers
before the room went dark."

—Satchel Paige, legendary Negro League pitcher, on Cool Papa Bell

First Edition
3 5 7 9 10 8 6 4

Printed in the United States of America

Reinforced binding

Library of Congress Cataloging-in-Publication Data on file.
ISBN-13: 978-0-7868-0832-8
ISBN-10: 0-7868-0832-2

Visit www.hyperionbooksforchildren.com

Paintings on pages iii, 33, 43, 48-49, 64-65, and 67 based on photographs courtesy of the National Baseball Hall of Fame, Cooperstown, New York.
Paintings on gatefold based on photographs courtesy of the Negro Leagues Baseball Museum, Kansas City, Missouri.
Painting on page 62 based on a photograph courtesy of Amereon House, Mattituck, New York.

"Jackie was an excellent choice because of his intelligence. That,
put together with his ability, made him a natural."

—Chet Brewer, pitcher for the Kansas City Monarchs, on Jackie Robinson

"I don't break bats, son."

"Baseball got me outta that celery field."
— John Jordan "Buck" O'Neil, first baseman for the Kansas City Monarchs

For Buck O'Neil, an inspiration

I wear them out."
—Josh Gibson, catcher for the Homestead Grays

"He'd cut your throat up here with a fastball."

— Frank Forbes, Negro League umpire, on Smokey Joe Williams

"Baseball is like everything else. You got to study every angle to win."

— Judy Johnson, third baseman for the Hilldale Daisies

"If we had played according to the money we made, I guess none of us would have been ballplayers long."

— Gene Benson, outfielder for the Philadelphia Stars

"We are the ship; all else the sea."

—*Rube Foster, founder of the Negro National League, owner of the Chicago American Giants*

FOREWORD

From the time I can remember, baseball has been my passion. Even when I did not have a bat and ball to play with, my friends and I learned to improvise. We made baseballs out of old rags or balled-up tin cans, and we played with broomsticks for bats and hit bottle tops for practice. Little did I know then that I was preparing myself to one day play in the major leagues.

I was honored when I received the call from supertalented artist Kadir Nelson, asking me to write the foreword for his new book. *We Are the Ship: The Story of Negro League Baseball* pays tribute to the men and women whose hard work and dedication helped black players like me make it into the big leagues. Kadir's powerful paintings eloquently bring this era to life and speak volumes about the old Negro Leagues.

Of course, I was reminded that during the twenties, thirties, and most of the forties, the Negro baseball leagues were the only teams that a black baseball player could aspire to play for. While many of us daydreamed about playing major league baseball, it was not until Jackie Robinson integrated the majors that I began to think that maybe there was hope for me. Up until Jackie signed with the Brooklyn Dodgers, I had set my sights on what was available to me—the Negro Leagues.

I traveled with the Indianapolis Clowns up and down the East Coast by bus, sometimes playing two or three games a day. We played baseball almost every day, practically living on the bus. Some of the older players would tell stories to us rookies about the legendary ballplayers who had played in the Negro Leagues, like Satchel Paige, "Cool Papa" Bell, and the mighty batter Josh Gibson.

After a few months with the Clowns, I was offered a spot with the major league Boston Braves. It was an opportunity I wasn't about to pass up. I signed with the Braves farm team that spring and was called up to the majors after they moved to Milwaukee two years later. I had finally realized my dream. I knew that if I wanted to stay around, being a black ballplayer, I had to do twice as much and work twice as hard. I felt I owed it to myself, to Jackie Robinson, and to all of those black players who came before me to give it everything I had.

Although I played in the Negro Leagues for a relatively short time, the experience meant a lot to me because it gave me an opportunity to play high-class baseball and develop my skills as a professional. When I read these stories and look at the artwork, I am flooded by memories of years past and grateful for Kadir's fresh approach to the subject. I know that I wouldn't have made it in baseball had these legends not paved the way for me.

—Hank Aaron

Atlanta, Georgia
May 2007

Hank Aaron, Milwaukee Braves

1st INNING

BEGINNINGS

"I ain't ever had a job, I just always played baseball."—Satchel Paige

Seems like we've been playing baseball for a mighty long time. At least as long as we've been free. Baseball's the best game there ever was. It's a beautifully designed game that requires a quick wit, a strong body, and a cool head.

They say baseball was invented by a fellow named Abner Doubleday in Cooperstown, New York, back in the mid-1800s, but that is just another tall tale, 'cause no one really knows for sure. But one thing *is* for sure: soon after that, you could find a baseball game being played just about everywhere in this grand ol' country of ours. Particularly in the big cities like New York and Chicago. People of all types loved to play and watch the game: Irish, Italian, German, Cuban, Puerto Rican, and African American (but back then we were called Negro or colored). Every neighborhood and every town had a team, and they would all play one another. Before long, there were professional teams and organized leagues.

In the mid-1860s, most professional baseball teams had only white ballplayers. There were a number of Negroes who did play, though they weren't treated any better than most Negroes in the country at the time. Truth is, those poor fellows were treated downright disgracefully. They were called just about every horrible name in the book, and then some. Several teams wouldn't play another team if it had a Negro on the roster; and in some states, Negroes weren't allowed to play at all. When we *did* play, we got the wrong directions from our manager and were targets for opposing pitchers and base runners, which was a dangerous thing, because back in those days, no one wore any type of protective gear—not even the catcher. Well, that was until Bud Fowler, the first Negro to play professional baseball, came

1

"Smokey" Joe Williams

MOSES · FLEETWOOD · WALKER

CHARLIE GRANT

SOL WHITE

PETE HILL

along. Too many times he was forced to leave the field on crutches after being spiked by a base runner. Now, this was a terrible thing, but some good came out of it. His scarred shins gave him the idea to attach wooden staves from a barrel to his legs for protection. They were the first shin guards and the first protective gear in baseball. They just about saved his legs and his baseball career—or what was left of it, anyway. And don't you know that those white fellows tried like the dickens to break his shin guards. It just gave them a little more ambition to slide feet first when a Negro was covering the base.

Despite the cruel treatment Negroes received, there were a few who became quite good ballplayers. Like brothers Welday and Moses Fleetwood Walker, Charlie Grant, Pete Hill, Sol White, Grant "Home Run" Johnson, Ben Taylor, and Frank Grant. These fellows were great ballplayers by any measure. But none of that mattered, 'cause they were still Negroes, and most white ballplayers didn't want to play alongside them.

By the late 1800s, Negroes began to disappear from professional baseball teams and were soon gone from them altogether. Now, there was never any written rule that prohibited Negroes from playing professional baseball, but soon after 1887, somehow Negroes all over couldn't *get* on a professional baseball team.[1] Come to find out that all the white owners had gotten together in secret and decided to do away with Negroes in professional baseball. They agreed not to add any more to their

FRANK GRANT

BUD FOWLER

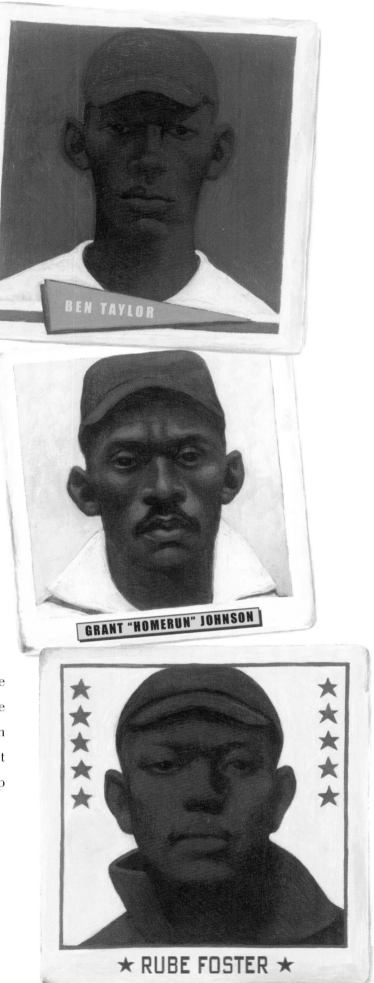

BEN TAYLOR

GRANT "HOMERUN" JOHNSON

★ RUBE FOSTER ★

teams and to let go of the ones they had. Called it a "gentlemen's agreement." And I'll tell you this, the white pro–ball-club owners held to that agreement for almost sixty years.

So, what were we Negroes left to do? We loved to play baseball, and a lot of guys had genuine talent. Sure, we could play against small semi-pro teams, which paid little, if at all; or swallow our pride and get a job working in some factory, but who wanted to do that? Especially after tastin' the fruits of what professional baseball had to offer. We had no choice but to start our own professional teams—our own leagues.

And that's just what we did.

In the early 1900s, there were many Negro baseball teams all over the Northeast and the South. Soon after the Great Migration of Negroes from the southern states to northern cities during the twenties, Negro baseball began to grow. Negroes tried several times to organize professional leagues, but they never lasted long because they didn't have the money or the leadership to stay in business.

Then came Rube.

Andrew "Rube" Foster was an old-time trick pitcher who'd come up from the Texas leagues. He was a preacher's son who called everybody "darlin'." Like most ballplayers in his day, he bounced 'round from team to team before he landed in Chicago with the Leland Giants (who later became the Chicago American Giants), where he both played and managed. Back then, managers almost always played, because the owners couldn't afford to pay a man to just sit in the dugout.

Rube was a master.[2] A brilliant man. He knew baseball like the back of his black hand, and more important, he knew how to win. He was a demanding manager, and only wanted ballplayers who would follow his instructions. If a ballplayer didn't listen to Rube, he didn't last long. His players had to be able to bunt the ball into a hat—consistently! All of 'em were fast, and if they got on base, it was over. They'd steal your shirt. Rube's game was built around speed and his own invention called the "bunt-and-run." It was a simple play. They'd put a racehorse on first base, and the batter would bunt the ball down the third-base line. The runner would lead off the base with the pitch and be halfway around the bases by the time the ball hit the bat. The runner didn't stop at second and kept charging full speed toward third, which was left unguarded because the third baseman had to come in to pick up the ball. If the third baseman played behind the base, it was an automatic hit. If he came in, the runner slid safely into third. The play was just about impossible to defend against. It also worked if a man was on second, except the runner would run all the way home.[3] They did this for nine innings. And let me tell you something. Those fellows would bunt and run you to death. Drove pitchers crazy!

And the pitchers, they got their pitching instructions from Rube sitting in the dugout, not from the catcher, which was more common. He'd puff signals from his pipe or nod his head one way to signal a play. One puff, fastball. Two puffs, curveball. Things like that. They beat everybody that way. Rube's American Giants became the strongest Negro team in Chicago and the most famous independent team in the entire Midwest. Sometimes they even drew larger crowds than the local major league Cubs and White Sox.

Rube ran his ball club like it was a major league team. Most Negro teams back then weren't very well organized. Didn't always have enough equipment or even matching uniforms. Most times they went from game to game scattered among different cars, or sometimes they'd even have to "hobo"—which means hitch a ride on the back of someone's truck to get to the next town for a game. But not Rube's team. They were always well equipped, with clean, new uniforms, bats, and balls. They rode to the games in fancy Pullman cars Rube rented and hitched to the back of the train. It was something to see that group of Negroes stepping out of the train, dressed in suits and hats. They were big-leaguers.

5

Rube Foster

Rube Foster and his Chicago American Giants, circa 1920

Oct. 11th, 1924

UPPER
BOX SEAT

FIRST COLORED

MUEHLEBACH FIELD

EST. PRICE $1.33

Federal Tax   .23

TOTAL $1.56

SEC.   **32**

BOX

UPPER
BOX SEAT

Oct. 11th, 1924

WORLD SERIES

KANSAS CITY, MO.

K. C. MONARCHS
VS
HILLDALE CLUB

OPENING GAME

MACKEY   ALLEN   CAMPBELL   LEWIS   THOMAS   COCKRELL   BRIGGS   WARFIELD   STEVENS   LAMBERT

WORLD SERIES

KANSAS CITY, MO.

FOSTER   BOLDEN   SANTOP   WINTERS   CURRIE   LEE   CARR   C. JOHNSON   J. JOHNSON   RYAN

2nd INNING

A DIFFERENT BRAND OF BASEBALL: NEGRO LEAGUE GAME PLAY

"We played tricky baseball."—Cool Papa Bell, legendary Negro League outfielder

We had some white umpires from another league call our game, once. Those poor fellows didn't know what to do with themselves. They made so many mistakes, they came over and apologized after the game, said they couldn't help it. They'd never seen our type of baseball. Said if they played like we did in the majors, they'd have to make the parks bigger to seat all the fans.[1]

We played a different brand of baseball from the majors. Negro baseball was fast! Flashy! Daring! Sometimes it was even funny. But always very exciting to watch. People would come early to the ballpark just to see us practice. We would whip that ball around the infield with such precision, they'd applaud.

We took pride in our baseball. Brought our own style to the game, and named our teams to match. Called ourselves the the Baltimore Elite Giants, the Philadelphia Stars, the Birmingham Black Barons, the Cleveland Buckeyes, the New York Cubans, the Atlanta Black Crackers, and many more. And we could play like we invented the game.[2] Kept the fans on the edge of their seats. Turned singles into doubles and doubles into triples, just by running hard. We used Rube Foster's "bunt-and-run" game to perfection. They don't bunt much today, and it kills us.

Some guys would clown on the field. Throw the ball behind their backs and get the guy out at first. Or play shadow ball, where the infielders would whip an imaginary ball around the bases. If you didn't know any better, you'd have thought they had a real ball. That's how good they were. Lloyd "Pepper" Basset used to catch some games in a rocking chair. Willis Jones used to take a newspaper with a hole in it out to center field and pretend he was

Jackie Robinson steals home past Cleveland Buckeye catcher, Quincy Trouppe.

reading it. If his team was way ahead and the ball was hit out there, he wouldn't go after it. One of the other guys would have to kill himself trying to get it.[3] A lot of our guys didn't like all that comedy, because to us, baseball was serious business. It was our means of putting food on the table. But truth be told, some of that stuff was funny! There were a couple of guys, Reece "Goose" Tatum and Richard "King" Tut, who were with the Indianapolis Clowns. They had a routine where Goose played the dentist and Tut the patient. Tut would fill up his mouth with corn, and Goose would act like he was pulling on Tut's tooth, but it wasn't coming out. So Goose went and got a firecracker and lit it in Tut's mouth. As soon as it went off, Tut would jump up hollering, and spitting out that corn like his teeth were fallin' out.[4] Had people on their backs with laughter. They would do the same thing every night.

Most of that clowning was done in the early days of Negro baseball, before Rube founded the league. The teams that clowned were not allowed in the league, because their acts were too much like the buffoonery you would see in the movies. Back then, the movies made full-grown Negroes look like fools or children, always telling jokes or dancing. Most of the time it was white folks made up to look like Negroes. It was downright shameful. But still, people would come out to see Negro teams like the Indianapolis Clowns play. They were a good draw. They had some good players on that team, too. Did you know that the major league home-run champ Hank Aaron played with the Clowns before he went up to the majors?

We didn't really know how rough it was in the Negro Leagues until some of our guys went up to the majors. Play was a lot "nicer" there. In our league, everything was legal. We would do whatever it took to win. Pitchers threw anything and everything. Spitters, shine-balls, emery balls, cut balls—you name it. They cut that ball to pieces and had curveballs breaking about six feet! Throw a new white ball to the pitcher, and it would come back brown[5] from all the tobacco juice and what-have-you. You never knew what the ball was going to do once it left the pitcher's hand. And throwing at a batter was common. The pitcher would knock you down just to mess with your head. Look up at the umpire, and he'd just say, "Get up and play ball, son." That's why the batting helmet was invented. When Willie Wells was just a rookie, he found the ball was making its way toward his head a little more often than he liked, so he decided to wear an old miner's helmet when he stepped up to the plate. Boy, did they laugh at him! But today, you won't find a ballgame played without batting helmets.

Base runners would spike you in a minute. Some of those guys would spike their mother if she were blocking home plate. A catcher learned not to block the plate if a runner was coming home. Get in the runner's way, and he'd step on the catcher's foot or run him right over, knock all his gear clear off. Come sliding in with his cleats high. Runners could tear your uniform off with those spikes. Some of those guys would sit in the dugout before the game filing their spikes, look at you, and say, "This is for you."[6] Those guys were mean. And many of them loved to fight.

Oscar Charleston

Oscar Charleston was a mean son-of-a-gun. He would just about go looking for trouble. One time he snatched the hood off a Ku Klux Klansman. Jud Wilson loved to use his fists, too. Many close games ended with a fight.

We didn't really have any spring training. We had to learn on the field. By springtime, we had already been playing down in Cuba or Mexico all winter. There wasn't any break. Soon as spring hit, we had paying customers. Games would last only about two hours and fifteen minutes. Not like those long games they have today, which can go about three hours or more. None of that stepping in and out of the batter's box, or stopping to have a word with the manager. We came to play. The ball we played with was a Wilson ball, which wasn't as lively as the expensive ball they used in the majors. Could you imagine all the home runs Josh Gibson or Norman "Turkey" Stearnes would have hit if we'd had that kind of ball? And we bought our bats straight off the shelf. Major leaguers had theirs made.[7]

Umpiring wasn't always that great, either. Some of those guys wouldn't have known a strike from their left foot. At one time, the league had official umpires, but they couldn't travel with the teams. It was too expensive. A few of the umpires were former players. Pop Lloyd and Wilber "Bullet" Rogan used to ump later on in their careers. Those guys were tough. They *had* to be, with guys like Oscar Charleston and Jud Wilson in the league. At one game in Kansas City, there were three umpires. Rogan was behind home plate, and the other two were at first and third. A play took place at third base, and Rogan ran down the line. He called the man out, and the base umpire called him safe. They started to argue and got into a fight. Bullet Rogan pulled out a knife, and the other guy panicked and took off running toward the center-field fence and climbed over it. The next day it was in the papers. Rogan had a bad temper. We wouldn't argue too much with him about balls and strikes. Whatever he called you, you would just let that go. He was old, but he'd fight you anyway. Some guys even played with a gun in their uniforms. It was a rough league.

And stats? Well, some teams kept them. But it wasn't a consistent thing. Most guys kept their own stats, or if a player on the team was keeping them, a bit of the information was lost when he had to bat or play in the field. Occasionally, a local newspaper would send a reporter out to keep stats, but the papers wouldn't pay them to do it very often. Sometimes those guys would come late and have to ask around, "What happened in the first inning?" "Who did what?"[8] or they'd just make up the stats. Even when the stats were recorded, they weren't always phoned in, or it was too much to try to stop and find a mailbox on the road while we were headed for the next town. Shoot, the white papers wouldn't run our scores anyway. Stats weren't consistently kept until later, after Jackie Robinson went up to the majors.

Umpires Hurley McNair, Bert Gholston, and Wilber "Bullet" Rogan. Kansas City, Missouri, circa 1942

3rd INNING

LIFE IN THE NEGRO LEAGUES

"It was a rough life—ride, ride, ride, and ride."—Hilton Smith, pitcher

We played in a rough league. We had a number of really unsavory characters like Charleston or Jud Wilson to contend with, as well as pitchers who didn't have a problem throwing at us, but that was something we had accepted as part of the game. I think what made our time a bit harder than most is what we had to deal with in addition to that. White fans would call us names and throw stuff at us on the field, and we couldn't say a word. In some places we traveled to, we couldn't get a glass of water to drink, even if we had money to pay for it—and back then, water was free!

We did an awful lot of traveling, mostly in buses. They were nice buses to begin with, but they weren't the kind that were made for ridin' every day.[1] We ran those poor buses ragged. Many a time we'd ride all day and night and arrive just in time to play a game. Then we'd get back on that hot bus and travel to the next town for another game, often without being able to take a bath. I gotta say, that cramped bus would get pretty ripe on some of those summer nights after a doubleheader. Phew! This was all season long. All of that traveling would wear on you. Many times the only sleep we got was on the bus. But that could be hard because we had to take the back roads to get to some of those little towns, and they were so bumpy they'd have us bouncing around the bus like popcorn on a hot stove. Fastest we could go was about thirty-five to forty miles an hour. If the driver got sleepy, a couple of the guys on the team would take turns driving the bus. To pass the time we played cards or sang old Negro spirituals or barbershop numbers. Just about every team had a quartet. They'd be our entertainment for most of the way. Some guys could really sing. Most people don't know it, but Satchel Paige had a wonderful singing voice, and so did Buck Leonard. We would listen to them and try to join in.

23

Newark Eagles owners, Abe and Effa Manley, enjoy the five-part harmony of their players on a bus ride to a game.

Traveling was even rougher down South. They didn't take too kindly to black folks down there—especially if you were from up north. We would have to travel several hundred miles without stopping because we couldn't find a place where we could eat along the way. It's a hurtful thing when you're starving and have a pocket full of money but can't find a place to eat because they "don't serve Negroes." And you could forget about trying to use the restroom in those places. You would just have to hold it, or stop the bus and do your business in the woods. We had to get used to it. After a while, we learned which places we could stop at and which ones we couldn't. They didn't have any fast-food places back then. Many times we wouldn't get food to eat before a game, and if we did, it usually wasn't much. We would have to play a doubleheader on only two hot dogs and a soda pop. If we couldn't buy food from a restaurant or a hot dog stand, we'd stop at a grocery store and get some sandwiches or sardines and crackers. Sometimes those grocery store clerks didn't want to serve us, either. One time a store clerk told us to put our money in an ashtray if we wanted to buy something. He grabbed the money out of the ashtray and put the change back in it. He didn't want to touch our hands, but he sure did touch that money. I guess he had to draw the line somewhere. Just didn't make any sense.

It was segregated in the North, too. They wouldn't serve us inside a restaurant, so we had to get our food from the back door and eat on the bus. We'd send one guy to buy food for the whole team. Hotels were segregated, too. Many times we would get to a town after riding all day, only to spend a few more hours searching for a place to stay. The minute we arrived, inexplicably, every hotel would be full. If we couldn't find anyplace to stay, we would have to sleep on the bus.

Some of the smaller clubs slept crammed in their cars or even in the ballpark because they couldn't afford to stay in a hotel. Some teams slept at the YMCA, the local jail, even in funeral homes. In cities, we stayed in Negro hotels or Negro rooming houses. We slept two, three guys to a bed. That's all the team owner could afford. A number of the Negro hotels were very clean and neat. But more than a few times, we'd run into those places—and I won't call out any names—that had so many bedbugs you'd have to put a newspaper between the mattress and the sheets.[2] And then in other places, we had to sleep with the lights on because the bedbugs would crawl all over you when the lights were out.[3] Can't sleep with a bug on your leg—I don't care how tough you are.

In small towns we'd stay with local families. During the game, the manager would send someone to find people who would put us up for the night. By the time the game was over, we all had places to stay. Sometimes the colored church would fix us a meal, and I'll tell you, that was some good eating.

If we got to a town and we had a little time to kill, we'd go fishing or catch a movie. Back then, a movie ticket only cost about twenty-five cents, and you could stay in the theater all day if you wanted to. We had to go through

24

Beautifully designed signage with a not-so-beautiful reminder of segregated times

Bronzville Inn
CABINS
—FOR—
COLORED

the back entrance, though, because they only allowed Negroes to sit in the balcony. There would usually be three levels in the theater, and the white audience would sit at the bottom. That whole middle section would be empty, as if the owners wanted us to be as far away from the white audience as possible. That kind of thing seems silly today, but that's how it was back then.

We played about 80 to 120 games during the regular season—the major league teams played about 154. The rest of the time we would barnstorm, which basically means that we played just about anybody and everybody who wanted to play a game, whenever and wherever we could get one. We barnstormed against professional and semipro teams all over the North, South, West, and the Midwest. Sometimes we played two, three, even four games in one day. For league games, we charged a dollar for the bleachers, two dollars for the grandstand, and two-fifty for box seats. But in those little towns, the admission was just fifty or seventy-five cents, and twenty-five cents for kids. We would average about fifteen or twenty dollars per player per game. That wasn't bad money. In those days you could do a lot more with a quarter than you can these days with a dollar. On some of those barnstorming trips, the smaller ball clubs slept on the side of the road in tents and had to catch their own food. The competition wasn't always very good in those little towns, either, but we had to be careful not to run the score up so high that we wouldn't be invited back.

On one occasion, Buck Leonard and his team couldn't play after they had traveled all day to get to this little town. When they got to the ballpark, they found out the Ku Klux Klan was marching there that night. They got back on the bus and blew out of there. I'll tell you what: back then, when the Klan was marching, Negroes went inside, turned out the lights, and pulled out a Bible.

Barnstorming through the South was nice at times. When we played in small black towns, people always treated it like it was a special occasion. For them, it was a big deal when a Negro League team came to town. It was like a family reunion. They would barbecue and play music. We had a grand ol' time. After the game, we'd go eat some of that good food and hang out with those nice folks before we had to jump on the bus again. It was in those towns that we'd find a lot of new ballplayers, too. They'd be playing wearing some ol' heavy shoes and raggedy uniforms, but many of those kids could throw like the devil and hit the ball a country mile! If they looked good enough, we'd bring them along with us. Had to make sure it was okay with their folks first, of course. We would also find new recruits when we played Negro college teams. In fact, that's where we found many of our rookie ballplayers. A good number of the guys in our league were college educated.

We played on some of the worst fields you could imagine. Once in a while, we'd play in a small town where they had just made the ballfield the same day we got there. Some ol' pasture. You had to pray the ball wouldn't land in some cow stuff. Some were so patchy—grass here, dirt there. Some didn't even have grass; and some were hard as

Willie Foster and young fans, Pittsburgh, Pennsylvania, circa 1952

a rock, with pebbles all over the place. You were always worried about the ball taking bad hops. Can't get to be a great fielder in those conditions. A few of our big Negro teams had their own parks, but most teams rented the big-league ballparks when the major league teams were away. Those big-league teams made good money renting their parks to us, but don't you know that after paying them all of that money to play in their ballpark, we still had to suit up down the street at the local YMCA or someplace else, because they didn't let us use the locker rooms?

Makes you mad to hear players today squawk about jet lag, and all of this. Try sleeping in a car with your knees to your chest, crammed with eight other guys, only to play a game the next day. Players today just don't know how bad it could be. We look back and wonder, "How did we do all of that?" It's simple. We loved the game so much, we just looked past everything else. We were ballplayers. There was nothing we would have rather spent our time doing.

Andy Cooper and the Detroit Stars play an exhibition game against a major league all-star team, circa 1920.

4th
INNING

RACKET BALL: NEGRO LEAGUE OWNERS

"Baseball really is an expensive thing to operate."—Effa Manley, co-owner of the Newark Eagles

In October 1929, the U.S. stock market crashed and sent the country spiraling downward into what is known as the "Great Depression." Businesses collapsed and banks closed, taking people's life savings with them. People were losing their jobs left and right, and soon it seemed everybody was out of work. What little money people had left could only be spent on food and heat. The Depression hit white baseball hard and Negro baseball even harder. The Eastern Colored League and the great Negro National League that Rube Foster had built fell apart after twelve seasons. Most teams disappeared. The teams that remained drifted around barnstorming wherever they could, passing the hat.

At the same time, Rube Foster was committed to a mental institution. Running the league and trying to keep everything together all those years had taken their toll on him. The Eastern League owners started raiding his league for players, and it sent him over the edge. Not long after that, he passed away. It was terrible to see this happen to such a great man. He did what no one else could do, and now all that he had worked for was gone. Within a very short time, the economy failed, the Eastern Colored League folded, and both Rube and his great Negro National League were laid to rest. It looked like the grand ol' days of the Negro Leagues were over.

Despite the hard times, there were a few who *did* make money during the Depression. They were known as "numbers men," racketeers. Some were intelligent black men who could have been stockbrokers or general managers of great corporations, but because of segregation, were not able to hold these positions. Instead, they found another

31

Gus Greenlee, owner of the Pittsburgh Crawfords

way to make big money—the "numbers" game. Back then, it was a 100 percent illegal business; but nowadays, it's known as the lottery, and it's run by the government. These numbers men went around town taking people's penny bets on predicting some random number from the stock market pages in the paper, or something like that. If you guessed the right number, depending on the odds, you could make some good money. But some of those guys wouldn't pay up if your number hit big, so people didn't always bet with them.

There was, however, one fellow who always made good on his bets. His name was Gus Greenlee. He was the king of the numbers game in Pittsburgh. He owned a bar called the Crawford Grill, where all the big Negro stars performed, from singing legend Lena Horne to Bill "Bojangles" Robinson, the great dancer and entertainer. Greenlee wore expensive suits and drove around town in his Duesenberg, a fancy car that in those days was worth a fortune. He also had a few fighters (one was none other than the world light heavyweight champ John Henry Lewis), and in 1930 he decided he was getting into the baseball business. It ended up being a great thing, because that fellow did a lot of good for Negro baseball. He picked up right where Rube left off. He reorganized the whole Negro National League and bought a team of his own, renaming it the Pittsburgh Crawfords.

Across town, there was a team called the Homestead Grays. They were a strong ball club that had come up from the steelworker leagues, but by this time, they were struggling because of the Depression. Like most folks, the owner, Cumberland Posey, needed money and was forced to sell off some of his best players. Gus Greenlee bought them all with a big smile and put together possibly one of the greatest teams in the history of baseball. It was a team of all-stars: Josh Gibson (the black Babe Ruth); William Julius "Judy" Johnson, a star third baseman; Ted Page, an outstanding outfielder; Ted "Double-Duty" Radcliffe, who used to pitch the top half of a doubleheader and catch the bottom half; and Jake Stephens. And to add to that: Satchel Paige (the most famous Negro League pitcher of all time) and James "Cool Papa" Bell (the fastest man in all of baseball). If that wasn't enough, he got the great Oscar Charleston to play with and manage them. It was a powerhouse. Five of those guys wound up in the Baseball Hall of Fame in Cooperstown, New York. Man, that team was unbeatable! Well . . . they *were* unbeatable, until Greenlee's numbers business got him into some trouble with the law. Someone on the inside of his operation had started to leak information to the police, and Gus ended up on the run. After that, his star players jumped the team to go play ball down in Santo Domingo. That was the end of the mighty Pittsburgh Crawfords.

Baseball was an expensive business to operate. Many of the owners made their money in the numbers business and used it to support their baseball teams, like Abe and Effa Manley, who owned the Newark Eagles. You also had Alex Pompez, owner of the Cuban Stars and the New York Cubans, and "Sonnyman" Jackson, who had a stake in the Homestead Grays. But there were also doctors, a few black celebrities, and even a couple of undertakers. World-

The Pittsburgh Crawfords

famous trumpeter Louis Armstrong had his "Secret Nine" ball club, and Bill "Bojangles" Robinson partly owned the New York Black Yankees. The world heavyweight boxing champ Joe Louis had a softball club; and Cab Calloway, the swing orchestra conductor, had his team of all-stars—and sometimes he even played, too. We knew many of the black entertainers and celebrities personally. It really wasn't a thing to see Lena Horne or Count Basie in the same hotel where we were staying. We went to see their shows after a game, and sometimes we would have dinner with 'em. They were on the road as much as we were, and they had to stay in the same Negro hotels and rooming houses. Some folks called it the "Chitlin' Circuit."

Most owners didn't make much money from their teams. Baseball was just a hobby for them, a way to make their illegal money look good. To save money, each team would only carry fifteen or sixteen players. The major league teams each carried about twenty-five. Average salary for each player started at roughly $125 per month back in '34, and went up to $500–$800 during the forties, though there were some who made much more than that, like Satchel Paige and Josh Gibson. The average major league player's salary back then was $7,000 per month. We also got around fifty cents to a dollar per day for food allowance. Back then, you could get a decent meal for about twenty-five cents to seventy-five cents.

Some of the owners didn't treat their players very well. Didn't pay them enough, or on time. That's why we would jump from team to team. Other owners would offer us more money, and we would leave our teams and go play for them. We were some of the first unrestricted free agents.

There were, however, a few owners who *did* know how to treat their ballplayers. Cum Posey was one of them. He always took care of his ballplayers, put them in the best hotels, and paid them well and on time. Buck Leonard said Posey never missed a payday in the seventeen years he played for the Grays. Gus Greenlee built his team a ballpark—first ballpark ever built for a Negro team. After home games, his players would go to his restaurant to have dinner and meet the pretty girls who were already there waiting for them. (Women have always loved ballplayers, you know.) Gus also gave some of his ballplayers jobs during the off-season. He even bought a team bus and printed Pittsburgh Crawfords on the side. Abe and Effa Manley heard about it and bought one for their team, too. Effa was a sweetheart. A real smart lady, and not bad on the eyes, either. She always made sure her players looked good, on and off the field. Had those boys looking sharp, with their suits and hats. Shoes shined like mirrors. Her husband, Abe, was a nice fellow, too. He always traveled with the team. Not every owner did that.

J. L. Wilkinson, who owned the Kansas City Monarchs, was one of the few white owners in Negro baseball. Like Rube Foster, he ran his team like it was a big league ball club. Did you know his team was the first to play night games in professional ball? In 1930, the Monarchs had the first portable lighting system in organized baseball. The

Night game, circa 1932

major leagues didn't begin playing night games until 1935. Night baseball changed everything. All those folks who had to work during the day were now able to see a baseball game in the evening. While it was still light, the players set the lights up on poles around the field next to first and third base and in the outfield. They had these big dynamos hooked up to generators run by a 250-horsepower engine housed in a truck parked way in the outfield. Sometimes the lights would dim, and we'd have to stop for a few minutes until the generators kicked back up again. They weren't really bright enough to play a baseball game, but we would play anyway. It was really hard to see the ball. If a fly ball was hit above the lights, you would have to pray it would find your glove or else you just got out of the way! We also used to have trouble with outfielders running into the poles chasing fly balls.[1] Some pitchers had the best games of their careers pitching night games. We'd put a long piece of white canvas along the center-field fence, so the batter could see the ball better coming over the plate.

A lot of people would come out for those night games. Night baseball was good for the league. It meant another payday for everybody. But it also made our lives tougher, because it meant we could play three, even four games a day instead of two. Satchel was right when he said, "We were worked. Worked like the mule that plows the field during the week and pulls the carriage to church on Sunday morning." [2]

Wilber "Bullet" Rogan

We had another fellow, Jud Wilson. Mean fellow. Real big upper body and little ol' legs. His knuckles were just about in the dirt. He scared the daylights out of pitchers. He crowded the plate and wouldn't back off. Just let the ball hit him so he could get on base. He could hit that long ball, too. But he had a bad temper. Always got into fights. He used to bully everybody, even the umpires. If they made a call he didn't agree with, he would go after them. Chase those poor fellows all around the field.

Oscar Charleston was one of the greatest ballplayers, black or white, in the history of the game. Certainly one of the best in his day. Many of the old-time white ballplayers who played against him would agree. He was like Hall of Famer Ty Cobb. He played *hard* and would do anything to win. He would run right over you if you were blocking the base. Cut you with his spikes. And that fellow was strong! Once he tore the steering wheel off a car. He could grab a baseball and loosen up the leather with his bare hands. He played center field, and stood right behind second base. If the ball was hit over his head, he'd run back and get it. He'd just outrun the ball![2] And could hit to all fields. Fans would chant "Charlie, Charlie, Charlie!"[3] when he came to bat. Didn't matter where it was pitched, he'd get wood on it. No pitch was a bad pitch, to him.

Buck Leonard was the same way. Couldn't get a ball past him. Some called him the "Black Gehrig." He was one of our finest all-around players. Real clean fellow. Didn't smoke or curse. He had a real nice swing. You could always count on him getting on base. He killed fastballs. And was an excellent first baseman.

Dick Seay and Newt Allen were two of our best second basemen. And Pop Lloyd was one of the most superb all-time shortstops in the world. They nicknamed him "The Black Wagner." In Cuba they called him "El Cuchara" (The Shovel), because he had big hands. He would scoop up grounders, dirt and everything, and zing 'em to first base. Willie Wells was an excellent shortstop, too. Both of those guys are in the Hall of Fame.

Ray Dandridge was one of our top third basemen. He was real flashy. Quite a showman. He would scoop up the ball and throw it all in one motion. We called him "Squatty" because he was so bowlegged. You could drive a train through his legs, but not a baseball.[4]

Judy Johnson was an outstanding third baseman, too. He would charge the ball. He wasn't as flashy as Dandridge, but he always got the job done. And was a very smart fellow.

In the outfield, we had Ted Page, Jimmie Crutchfield, Turkey Stearnes, and of course, Cool Papa Bell, who was the fastest man in *all* of baseball. He was like lightning. Cool Papa could circle the bases in twelve to thirteen seconds. One minute he was standing still on first base, and next thing you know, he was slowing up at third. More than once he scored from first base on a bunt. He was so fast, Jesse Owens, the Olympic sprinter, wouldn't race him without his track shoes. And he was always in shape. Never had to worry about him getting tired. He could hit, and had

William Julius "Judy" Johnson

The mighty Josh Gibson watches Satchel Paige pitch to Buck Leonard. Griffith Stadium, Washington, D.C., circa 1943

a good arm. Many folks don't know he used to be a pitcher, an old knuckleballer. He was a real quiet fellow, too. He wouldn't argue at all. That's why they called him "Cool Papa"—because he was so easygoing.

Behind the plate we had highly skilled catchers like "Pepper" Basset, Josh Gibson, Quincy Trouppe, and Roy Campanella. But Raleigh "Biz" Mackey was possibly the greatest defensive catcher in Negro League history. Roy Campanella, the catcher who played with Jackie Robinson on the Brooklyn Dodgers, learned everything he knew about catching from Mackey. When you saw Campy's moves behind the plate, you were seeing Mackey. He was a great technician. Handled pitchers with ease and could throw to second base from a crouch. Couldn't fool around with him. *Nobody* would try to steal on Biz. He'd throw you out. He didn't drop many balls, either. Especially fly balls. He didn't even take off his mask to catch 'em. Solid hitter, too.

On the mound we had fireballers like Smokey Joe Williams, Willie Foster (Rube's younger brother), Andy Cooper, Hilton Smith, Verdell Mathis, Cannonball Dick Redding, Bullet Rogan, Leon Day, and many others. But the most famous of all pitchers was Leroy "Satchel" Paige. He got his nickname "Satchel" when he was a boy. He used to work at the train depot, carrying folks' bags and satchels. Satchel was a masterful pitcher, and by far the greatest showman. People came out by the thousands to see him pitch. If a team needed some cash, Wilkinson would send him out there to pitch a few innings for them. Satchel made a lot of money doing that. He pitched for more than 250 teams. That fellow was something else. We'd be waiting around for Satchel to show up for a game, and he was nowhere to be found. Then he'd arrive just a few minutes before game time with a police escort, sirens blazing and all. He always kept us laughing. He would walk real slow to the mound and let his long arms dangle. Satchel didn't believe in running. A few times he called in the outfield and struck out the side without giving up a single hit. He was tall and skinny. If he turned sideways, he'd disappear. His arms were just as skinny around his biceps as his wrists. We used to say they were like rubber hoses, or long black snakes.

Nowadays, pitchers pitch maybe once or twice a week and rest a few days in between. Not Satchel. He pitched every day. He lived on that mound. He said he kept his arm young by taking boiling hot showers. He would tie a big Turkish towel around his arm and let the hot water run over it. Nowadays, pitchers use ice for their arms; but back then, they used heat. He also rubbed his arm with this real hot snake oil that some American Indian fellow gave him. He wouldn't give up that secret formula for anything. When Satchel pitched, he raised his big foot up high, let it come down, and then whipped the ball by you. Satchel was nothing but fastball. Even his slow stuff was fast. We knew what was coming, but we still couldn't hit it. The ball would be moving so fast it looked like a little white pill by the time it got to the plate. And it would jump just a little bit before it got to you, just enough to make you miss it. Satchel wasn't legendary only for his speed, but also for his control. He could put the ball wherever he wanted to

Raleigh "Biz" Mackey

Leroy "Satchel" Paige, Yankee Stadium, Bronx, New York, circa 1942

put it. Most pitchers warmed up by throwing over home plate or a glove, but Satchel used a candy wrapper or a bottle cap. A catcher only had to hold up his glove, and Satchel would hit it.

Satchel liked to drive fast, too. Drove like a demon! He'd get stopped for speeding in some small towns on his way to a game. Once he got stopped and the judge fined him twenty-five dollars. Satchel took out a wad of cash and started peeling off ten-dollar bills. Told the judge, "Here's fifty, I'm coming back through tomorrow."[5] Yeah, that Satch was something else.

One of Satchel's rivals at the plate was Josh Gibson. Josh was hitting that ball out of ballparks everywhere. He hit more home runs than anybody except Turkey Stearnes. Some say Josh hit the ball out of Yankee Stadium. (Not even Babe Ruth did that.) He had the most beautiful, natural swing. His body was built for hitting. Slender waist. Big muscular back. He would roll his sleeves up so the pitcher could see his powerful arms. He stood flat-footed, and would just mash the ball. The ball would shoot straight toward the outfield and still be on its way up as it cleared the fence. It would land about 400 or 500 feet away. If an infielder had tried to catch it before it took off, the ball would have probably taken him with it! Josh hit everything: fastballs, curveballs. Couldn't fool him. Pitchers would just have to pitch and pray. He was so good, people started calling him "Mr. Black Baseball."[6] Some even called him the "Black Babe Ruth," but others say that the Babe should have been called the "White Josh Gibson." Josh was a real jolly fellow. We used to say he was like a big kid. And great behind the plate, too. When he started out, he wasn't as good a catcher as he was a hitter. But he wanted to become a complete player, so he really worked hard on developing his arm and, most of all, his accuracy. He became one of the better defensive players. He could pick you off at second from a crouch. The man was awesome.

But you know something? We had many Josh Gibsons in the Negro Leagues. We had many Satchel Paiges. But you never heard about them. It's a shame the world didn't get to see them play. The Negro Leagues were home to some of the greatest baseball players that ever lived. Guys like Stuart "Slim" Jones, John Beckwith, Dick Lundy, and Oliver Marcelle. Newt Allen, Dobie Moore, Jimmie Crutchfield, "Pepper" Basset, Dan and Sam Bankhead, Buck O'Neil, Bingo DeMoss, Joe Black, Roy Partlow, Ted Page, Alex and Ted "Double Duty" Radcliffe, Chet Brewer, Quincy Trouppe, Andy "Pullman" Porter, Piper Davis, Walter McCoy, "Mule" Miles, "Wild Bill" Wright . . . there were just so, so many. Can't even name them all. Unfortunately, most of them will never receive the recognition they deserve. We can only hope the Baseball Hall of Fame in Cooperstown will someday open the doors to more of these fellows.

Norman "Turkey" Stearnes

6th INNING

LATIN AMERICA: BASEBALL IN PARADISE

"The crowds were big and the fans red-hot."—"Schoolboy" Johnny Taylor, pitcher, New York Cubans

Many ballplayers in the Negro Leagues came from Latin America. Baseball was real popular down there in Cuba, Mexico, Puerto Rico, the Dominican Republic, and Venezuela. It was so warm, they could play baseball all year long. And they did. Those fellows became quite good and had some *strong* teams. Quite a few of those boys could have made a fortune if they had played in the majors. Martin Dihigo was one of them. Baseball came to him just as natural and easy as breathing. He could play every position—even pitch. Had natural grace, like Joe DiMaggio. He was really something to watch. José Méndez was a great pitcher and played all positions, too. Another fellow, Cristóbal Torriente, he was known as the "Black Christy Mathewson." They say he could hit the ball over a mountain. If he had been a couple shades lighter, he could have played in the majors. Major league owners would take a Cuban before they would a Negro. Guess they didn't know slave ships stopped down in those islands, too.

Some of the Latin ballplayers didn't want to play in the United States anyway. They didn't want to leave their home—and who could blame 'em? It was nice down there. It was always warm, and those Latin women sure were pleasing to the eye. And they loved Americans. Down there, Negroes were treated just the same as anyone else, the way we were supposed to be treated. There was no such thing as segregation. We could stay at any hotel and eat at any restaurant. And if you were a ballplayer, a good ballplayer, they treated you like a king. Kids followed us in the streets asking for autographs. Our pictures would be in the newspaper. The Latin ball club owners paid for our plane tickets—both ways—and put us up in hotels for the whole winter. We could even bring our families if we wanted

53

Willard Brown and fans celebrate a victory. Santurce, Puerto Rico, 1940s

Martin Dihigo

to. Didn't have to pay for a thing. And we traveled to games by train, not on those old bouncy, rickety buses. We only had to play about three, maybe four games a week, mostly on the weekends. That was heaven compared to the Negro Leagues. The rest of the time we would go fishing, go to a cantina, or hang out in those plazas, do some girl watching. In

Mexico, we would even go to bullfights. The Latin Leagues paid well, too, much more than the Negro Leagues. You could fill up a whole trunk full of those pesos.[1] That's why a lot of guys would jump the Negro League teams to go play down there. It drove the Negro League owners crazy. Satchel Paige almost broke up the whole Negro League when he took a bunch of stars down there to play. Wiped out poor Gus Greenlee's Crawfords. The Negro Leagues banned Satch after that—well, for a little while, anyway.

But in Latin America, you had to produce. If you didn't play well, they put you right back on the plane and sent you home. Two, maybe three bad games, then you were out of there. They were serious about their baseball. Fans were crazy, too. Never seen fans get so excited about a baseball game. Go to town after a bad game, and they wouldn't speak to you. They'd just look at you mean. And, man, they went wild if you hit a home run. In Cuba, they would give you beer or money if you hit one. They'd give you a car in Puerto Rico if you hit twenty-five of 'em. That's right, a car. A Hudson. But it was hard to hit home runs in some of those parks. They were huge! Many long balls that should have been home runs were caught. And if you were a pitcher, you couldn't throw at batters like we used to. Hit one of their batters, and they'd throw you in jail.

And boy, was it hot down there! You could see the heat coming off the ground! Had to keep moving in the outfield, 'cause the heat would burn up through the bottoms of your shoes. Some guys passed out in the field, even in the dugout. It was so hot that the first game of a doubleheader would be in the morning and the second game wouldn't be till late afternoon when it was cooler. The food was even hotter. If you didn't ask them to take it easy on the spices, they would load that food up, and it would burn right through you. Satchel Paige blamed his stomach miseries on all of that hot food that he ate while he was down there. (The truth was, it was his rotten teeth.)

We had some great games playing against those Latin fellows. We were all good friends. We would hang out and play cards after the game or go fishing together. We had a good time. But as soon as we put on those uniforms and walked onto the field, we didn't know each other. They'd spike you like you were a stranger. One time, Ted Page was playing in Cuba. He was fooled on a pitch he thought was a curveball and was hit in the head with the ball. Knocked him out cold. When Page came to, he looked up at the pitcher, and instead of asking him if he was okay, that pitcher said, "You not hit that one too good."[2] You didn't get any sympathy from them. We were the same way.

It was a lot of fun playing down there, but sometimes it would get lonely. They treated us nice and it was really beautiful, but after a while we'd get a little homesick. There was always a language barrier, and their cultures were so different from ours. Playing in Latin America was a great way to spend the winter; but ask anybody, it is tough going without a plate of greens, sweet candied yams, and some buttermilk biscuits for four months. We knew when it was time to go home.

7th INNING

GOOD EXHIBITION:
THE NEGRO LEAGUES VS. THE WHITE LEAGUES

"When we played head-to-head it was nip-and-tuck. They won some and we won some."
—Gene Benson, outfielder for the Philadelphia Stars

Our season started in the spring and ended in September. We played more than a hundred games a season, and then played winter ball in Cuba or Mexico. In between we traveled all over the country playing all kinds of teams— black, white, Latin, pro and semipro. Some Negro Leaguers even barnstormed in Canada and Asia, but most games were played in the United States. In many places, we wouldn't see a black face for miles around. The home team would supply the umpires, usually the town sheriff or somebody like that. The winner would get sixty percent of the gate, and the loser forty. If we tied, we'd split it even down the middle. They did their best to keep us from winning, sometimes dragging the game out until it was too dark to play to force a tie. We had more ties than anything.[1] We could've beaten most of those teams with our hands behind our backs, but we would get robbed. The umpires would call us out when we were safe and everything was a strike, no matter where it was pitched. You'd have thought all of their pitchers were named Satchel Paige. We had to learn to hit bad pitches. The Brooklyn Bushwicks used to freeze the balls before the game, took the life out of 'em. When we hit 'em, they wouldn't go very far.

Sometimes we would get *them*, too. There was a catcher, Chappy Gray, who used to catch Satchel when he was in his prime. One time they were playing in Enid, Oklahoma. By the time the game got up into late innings, it started to get kinda dark. So Chappy told Satchel, "Hey, Satchel, you got two strikes on this hitter. Man, you throwin' the ball so hard, I can't see it too well and I don't want to break my finger. I'll tell you what you do. You wind up like you are going to throw the ball and I'll hit my fist in my mitt, make it sound like it's the ball. Man, nobody'll know the

57

difference." He told Satchel, "You don't want to hit one of these white guys, man, or we're gonna have to leave here runnin'! They'll hang us down here!" Satchel said, "Okay, I'll do that." So he went back out there and he wound up and came down with that long stride, big follow-through. Chappy hit his fist in his mitt, and the umpire yelled, "Strike three!" That hitter was so mad, he threw his bat down. He yelled at the umpire, "You blind, Tom?! Anybody who could see knows that ball was high and outside!"

Those little white towns in the South were rough. The fans would call you everything. One lady brought us a black cake. Had it delivered by a man in a white coat. Written with icing, from the top corner to the bottom corner at an angle, was spelled N-I-G- . . . etc. Now, why would somebody go through the trouble to do something like that? I guess you could call that dedication. Kids in those towns didn't know any better. They'd call you the N-word before they'd say "colored people" because it was easier.[1] And we couldn't talk back. Fight back, or even run the score up too high, they might chase us out of there, and we wouldn't get paid. It wasn't big money, but we needed it. You couldn't change those folks' minds anyhow. We were just a bunch of ballplayers. They were *long* set in their ways.

There were white teams who traveled just as much as we did. Life on the road was rough but wasn't as bad for them because they could stay where they played and didn't have trouble finding a meal. House of David was one of those teams. We played them quite often. They were a good ball team. They were from a religious colony out in Benton Harbor, Michigan. Wore long hair and beards. The major leagues frowned on facial hair back then. There were a couple of knockoff House of David teams, too. Sometimes they would hire major leaguers to play for them in the off-season. They would wear false beards when they played, but they weren't fooling anybody. Even ol' Satch pitched a few innings for the Colored House of David.

We played major leaguers quite often. When their season ended in October, they would barnstorm against us out in California, and sometimes in Cuba. We played everybody from Ty Cobb to Babe Ruth. We won about sixty percent of the time. We hit them just the same as we hit our own pitchers. And they had just as much trouble hitting Satchel as we did. That's how we knew we were good enough to play in the major leagues. There was never any problem on the field. We were friends with those guys. If there was a guy who didn't want to be bothered with us, then he just wouldn't play. The guys on the other team would come over after the game and tell us how good we were. Man, if we had a nickel every time we he heard, "If you were white, you'd be worth such-an'-such," we'd all be rich men. They knew we were just as good as they were. They respected us, and we respected them. A ballplayer is a ballplayer, and good ballplayers are always up for a good game. And we'd give it to 'em.

Besides, they made some good money playing against us. Back then, major leaguers didn't make all the money that they make today. In the off-season, they had to find a way to make a living.

We had a good thing going, playing the major leaguers in the off-season, until Stan Musial, the St. Louis Cardinal slugger, put an end to it unintentionally. He was supposed to play with the Cleveland Indians pitching great, Bob Feller, on an all-star barnstorming team out in California, only Musial started late because the Cardinals were in the World Series. That year the Series went seven games, and by the time Musial made it out to California, the Pacific Coast League had already started up. By the end of the season, he realized how much money he could have made had he been there the whole time, much more than he made in the World Series. He told people about it when he got home, and when Judge Kenesaw Mountain Landis, the commissioner of major league baseball, who was dead set against integration, caught wind of it, he made a rule that banned all major leaguers from barnstorming until the World Series was over. That Landis tried everything to stop those major leaguers from playing us. We were winning too many games, and he broke the whole thing up. Said something about the major league getting a "black eye" when we beat them.[2] He cut back the number of games they could play us and told them they couldn't wear their major league team uniforms. They had to call themselves "all-stars," and play down our games as mere "exhibitions."

Satchel Paige put together an all-star team, and played major league pitchers Bob Feller's and Jay Hanna "Dizzy" Dean's all-star teams. When people heard that Satchel Paige was gonna be pitching against Dizzy Dean or Bob Feller, they would come, like we used to say, "two to a mule."[3] One year, Diz and Satch filled Yankee Stadium for one of those exhibition games. They charged full price and made a killing! Sometimes Satchel was throwing so hard he wouldn't let their batters even *touch* the ball with the bat. And Feller and Dean—those boys could bring it, too.

As far as competition, I'd have to say we were about even. Only thing different was that they were a little more polished than we were, and those major league teams had deeper benches than we did. Negro League teams would only carry about fifteen to nineteen players at most, with about six pitchers—two good and the rest mediocre—and one good catcher. The majors would carry about twenty-five players: six or seven good pitchers and two good catchers. If we got hurt, well then, we just had to play hurt, 'cause there wasn't anyone to come in for us. We used to say, "We were paid for nine [innings], so we played for nine."[4]

But even with all that, we still won baseball games. I guess we beat those major leaguers as often as we did because we could out-think them. Baseball is a game of intelligence. For a long time, a lot of people thought Negroes could never play major league ball because they thought we weren't smart enough. It took them a long time to realize that *nothing* was further from the truth. Those major leaguers learned a lot by playing us, and we learned a lot by playing them. They learned we were men just as they were, and they would shake our hands and look us in the eye after we beat them, as did we. Maybe we did help change a few minds by playing baseball, after all.

Jay Hanna "Dizzy" Dean and Satchel Paige

East Negro League all-stars, East-West Classic, 1939. Comiskey Park, Chicago, Illinois

Toward the end of the war when players started to come back, crowds got bigger and bigger. Black folks would come by the thousands for a Negro League baseball game. Before and after the game, there would be lively music and food, and in bigger cities they would have beauty or swimsuit contests or "ladies' night." And on opening day, the ballparks would be "filled to the gills."[1] A black entertainer or the mayor would throw out the first pitch. Many times Negro League teams would outdraw the local major league teams. The Homestead Grays would have 30,000 people in the stands for a Sunday game[2] when the Washington Senators had only 25,000.

Although several of our teams lost players to the draft, Negro baseball was still good business, and with the help of night baseball, the leagues thrived during World War II. Players' salaries grew, and the *Saturday Evening Post* even did a big story on Satchel Paige. After that, anywhere he pitched, there was a huge crowd. He'd only have to pitch a few innings and then someone else, usually Hilton Smith, a great pitcher in his own right, would finish the game.

The *biggest* crowds could be found every August in Chicago's Comiskey Park at the East-West Classic, the Negro League's all-star game. It was founded by Pittsburgh Crawfords owner Gus Greenlee in 1933, the same year the major league had their first all-star game. Managers and owners elected players for the all-star teams, and fans voted for them in the black newspapers: the *Pittsburgh Courier*, the *Kansas City Call*, the *Baltimore Afro-American*, and the *Chicago Defender*. There was nothing more glorious than the East-West Game. People came from as far as Louisiana and Mississippi and Tennessee to see it. The railroad had to add extra cars to the trains just to make room for all of those folks traveling to the game. A couple of times we had more than 50,000 people crammed into that ballpark;[3] we had to turn people away. The East-West Game would even outdraw the major league all-star game. Look in the crowd, and there in the front row was Bill "Bojangles" Robinson, Joe and Marva Louis, Louis Armstrong, Billie Holiday, or Lena Horne. It became more than just a game, it was a high-class affair! People who didn't know anything about baseball came to the ballpark in their Sunday best just to be *seen* at the East-West Game, you hear? Black *and* white.

We had some *great* games, too. The score was usually close. Can you imagine Satchel Paige, Chet Brewer, Buck Leonard, Josh Gibson, Cool Papa Bell, and Mule Suttles all on the same team? The best in Negro baseball. All of 'em, down there, ready to give the people a show.

If the owners didn't do well during the season, they could make it up at the East-West Game. The players only got about fifty dollars each, and the rest, after expenses, went to the owners' pockets. They made out like bandits. Satch and Josh later negotiated their own fee, and soon the players banded together and demanded more money—and they got it.

And I'll tell you something. It wasn't until the major league owners saw all of those fans at the East-West Game that they started thinking a little more seriously about integrating baseball. The almighty dollar has a way of changing folks' minds.

Buck Leonard

9th INNING

THEN CAME JACKIE ROBINSON

"There was never a man in the game who could put mind and muscle together quicker and with better judgment than [Jackie Robinson]."—Branch Rickey

There is a story the pitcher Chet Brewer used to tell:

A black boy went into the ballpark and he told a white manager, "Hey, I'd like to try out for your team." The white manager said, "Go away, boy. I don't have any room for a black boy on my team." He went away and came back the next night and asked the manager again. The manager said, "I told you last night I don't have any room for a black boy on my team." So he came back a third night and the manager said, "I've had it up to here with you. If you come back tomorrow night, I'll have the police throw you in jail!" So the following night the kid bought a ticket right over this white man's dugout. And he sat there and he bugged this manager and he bugged him and he bugged him. So finally the manager said, "Hey, Coach! Get that man down here and give him a uniform. I'm gonna pick out a spot in this game to embarrass him so he won't ever come back. Because I know he can't play, he's just a lot of mouth." So he brought him down and put him in a uniform. And this particular night they were playing a team that had the ace relief pitcher in the whole league, a big giant of a white man who threw BB's. The opposing pitcher walked the bases full and the manager said, "This is where I'll show this black boy up." He said, "Hey, you! You pinch hit." So the kid ran by the bat stand, picked up the first bat he came to, and walked up to the plate. The opposing

69

manager summoned his big relief ace pitcher from the bullpen. And the first pitch this big white man threw, this black boy hit it up against the right center-field fence. And as he was rounding second base, the white manager jumped up and said, "Look at that Cuban go!"[1]

Major league owners had been looking at our Negro League players for years. It's no secret that some of 'em wanted to sign Negroes to their teams. They would try to pass 'em off as Cuban or American Indian. John McGraw, the manager of the Baltimore Orioles back in 1901, signed a Negro named Charlie Grant to his team. Now, everybody and his mother knew that Charlie was a Negro, but McGraw tried to pass him off as a Cherokee Indian named Chief Charlie Tokahama. It almost worked, too, until a bunch of Negroes went to congratulate him after a game and ruined the whole thing.

Toward the end of World War II, major league owners began sending their scouts to Negro League games. They even gave some of our guys tryouts, but nothing ever came of it. Even the last-place teams wouldn't take us. They always had some excuse like, "There are just too many of you to go in" or "Nobody wants to be the first one to sign a Negro." We knew that if they decided to sign one of us, it meant we'd be taking the place of one of the white ballplayers, and he'd be out of a job. That didn't sit too well with the major leaguers. It seemed like the major league owners would never sign a Negro ballplayer.

Kenesaw Mountain Landis made a statement in the papers saying there was no agreement of any sort that banned Negroes from playing in the majors, but how else do you explain the absence of Negroes from major league base-ball for almost sixty years? That statement was a flat-out lie. Landis wouldn't have let a Negro into the major leagues if his life depended on it, and that's the truth! Bill Veeck tried to buy the Philadelphia Phillies and planned to load the team up with Negro League stars like Josh Gibson, Cool Papa Bell, and Satchel Paige. He told Landis what he wanted to do, but of course, Landis shot it down. The team was sold to somebody else for next to nothing.

After nearly twenty-five long years as Major League Baseball Commissioner, Judge Landis died in 1944. A new commissioner was elected, A. B. "Happy" Chandler. A couple of reporters from the black papers immediately asked him where he stood on the question of integrating baseball. That fellow came right out and said, "If a colored boy can make it on Okinawa and Guadalcanal . . . he can make it in baseball."[2] We had waited more than fifty years to hear those words. It was all over the papers. People, black and white, were talking about it at the dinner table, in the street, in the barbershops, on the radio, in the newspapers—everywhere. A lot of the major league owners didn't like what Chandler said. Especially coming from a southern fellow—that really got him into some trouble. They couldn't wait for him to make a mistake. As soon as he stubbed his toe, Chandler was out of there.[3] He only lasted a few years as commissioner. But *he* made it possible for Negroes to play in major league baseball. People always talk about Branch

Rickey integrating baseball, and he deserves a great deal of credit because he was the only major league owner willing to take a chance on a Negro ballplayer; but if it hadn't been for Chandler, Rickey couldn't have done a thing.

After the door to the major leagues had finally opened, the only question was, "Who will be the first to go?" By that time, many of our great Negro League players were past their prime. Buck Leonard was about thirty-eight, thirty-nine years old. Ray Dandridge was up there, too, and so was Josh Gibson, and he was sick. Satchel and Cool Papa were even older. And if they had been called up, they wouldn't have gone straight to the majors. They would have had to play in the minors for a year or two. On top of that, they would have had to take a pay cut. Most guys were making about $800 a month in the Negro League, and that was good money. Starting salary in the minors was about half that.

The owners were looking for somebody young. We had a few young ballplayers who were good enough to choose from: Larry Doby, Monte Irvin, Roy Campanella, Jackie Robinson, and a few others. We thought Monte would have been the first to go, or maybe Larry Doby. But they chose Jackie Robinson. Why Jackie? Now, Jackie was a good ballplayer, but we had guys we thought were better. A lot of the guys weren't happy that Jackie was chosen to be first. But you know something? You can be wrong about a person. We look back and see that they found the right man in Jackie.[4] All of that stuff he took, nobody else would have taken. At most games, white fans hissed at him and spat at him, and once even threw a black cat on the field. I remember a bunch of the guys sitting around talking about Jackie and the stuff those white folks were doing to him while he was with the Montreal Royals. Josh Gibson said, "Man, if they did that to me, I would've punched them in the mouth!" And everybody said, "See! That's why you didn't go!"

Jackie was a big guy. About six feet, two hundred and five pounds. He had a college education and had played with whites while he was in school. And he was fast. He had been a track star out in California before he went into the military. So was his brother Mack, who placed second behind Jesse Owens in the 200-meter dash in Germany. Jackie had played football and basketball, too. On the Kansas City Monarchs he played shortstop and second base, and during his year with the team, he hit .345 with ten doubles, four triples, and five homeruns. Jackie *hated* to lose. He wouldn't take anything from anybody. I tell you, Jackie had a terrific temper[5] and could curse like a sailor! If he felt someone was doing him wrong, he would let him know about it. Jackie got into about three fights that year he was with the Monarchs. One was with an umpire. Knocked him out cold, but the players tried to keep that one quiet.[6] It was his temper that got him out of the service early. The military was segregated back then and it drove him crazy. Those guys would yell at Jackie, calling him this and that. That kind of thing was hard for a man like Jackie to take. He knew he was smarter than a lot of those guys and got himself into trouble talking back. Once, while he was riding a military bus, the driver told him to sit in the back where Negroes were *supposed* to sit. Jackie knew that on a military bus he could sit wherever he wanted, so he refused. Although the army officers knew he

was right, Jackie was court-martialed. He beat the charges but was later honorably discharged from the military.

But Jackie was a good man despite his temper. He didn't drink or smoke and wouldn't go out on the town chasing girls like most of the other fellows. He just stayed at the hotel and played cards. His heart belonged to one gal. He was so serious. We used to kid him about how serious he was. He always talked about playing in the majors. Maybe deep down, he knew he'd be the first to go. Even still, he was very nervous about being able to make it in the big leagues. His roommate on a barnstorming team in Venezuela, Gene Benson, said, "Where you're goin' ain't half as tough as where you been."[7] He told Jackie about how we had played major leaguers for years and beat them just the same as we had beaten our own teams, even though our playing conditions were so much tougher. Hearing that really helped Jackie.

Before Jackie signed with the major league team the Brooklyn Dodgers, the team owner, Branch Rickey, wanted to meet Jackie face-to-face. During the meeting, Mr. Rickey acted as if he was angry, yelling and calling Jackie every racial epithet in the book, just to test Jackie's famous temper! Jackie kept his cool and just sat there. He was probably wondering why this old white man called him all of these things when they were just supposed to be having a meeting. Mr. Rickey explained that he was only testing him and that this was the sort of thing he would have to face every day on the road, and that he would have to hold his temper and not talk back, no matter what, for a period of three years. He asked Jackie if this was something that he could do. Most guys would have said, "Oh yes, Mr. Rickey! I can do that!" But Jackie thought for a moment. Then he looked Mr. Rickey in the eye and said, "If you are willing to take this risk and allow me to join your ball club, I can assure you that there will be no incident." This really impressed Mr. Rickey, and it only shows just how smart and eloquent Jackie was.[8]

Jackie signed with the Brooklyn Dodgers in 1945. He played his first year with Montreal, the Dodgers' farm team, and led the team to the minor league World Series. In the spring of 1947, Jackie was called up to the Dodgers and did well there, too. He hit .297 and led his team with 29 stolen bases and 125 runs scored. He also had twelve home runs. The Dodgers won the pennant in 1947, and *The Sporting News* named Jackie rookie of the year. But the most amazing thing of all was that he did it under all that pressure. He received death threats, and someone even threatened to kidnap his little boy. On the field, the fans called him names and threw stuff at him. Pitchers threw at him, and players pushed him around and tried to spike him when they ran the bases. He had to deal with that kind of thing every single day. And the worst part was that he couldn't fight back. He didn't say anything, because he knew it would ruin the chances of any other Negro playing in the majors. I think that is what hurt Jackie the most. He was the type of guy who always stood up for himself and he just couldn't do that in the majors—at least for the first three years. He had to keep it all inside. That kind of thing can make you sick. That's why he died so young. Baseball is what killed Jackie. Nothing else.

But Jackie did something that made us all proud. He brought our Negro League style of play to the major leagues and changed the face of baseball. He made it quicker and more daring. His base running changed the way pitchers had to pitch. And most important, Jackie cleared the way for the rest of us to play in the majors, and in doing that, he helped bring the rest of the country closer to accepting Negroes as first-class citizens.

Ray "Squatty" Dandridge

Extra **I**NNINGS

THE END OF THE NEGRO LEAGUES

"If we get you boys, we're going to get the best ones. It's going to break up your league."
—Clark Griffith, owner of the major league Washington Senators

After Jackie crossed, it just about killed the Negro Leagues. Most everyone was happy to see Jackie go to the majors, but it really burned many of the owners. Major league owners began to sign many of our ballplayers but paid the Negro League owners next to nothing—if anything at all. J. L. Wilkinson, the owner of the Monarchs, didn't get a dime for Jackie Robinson or any of the other players he lost. The fans deserted the Negro Leagues when Negroes went up to the majors. They'd travel hundreds of miles to see black players on white teams, but wouldn't travel across town to see us. In 1946, the Homestead Grays drew about 30,000 people to a Sunday game. After '47, they only drew 300. Their first baseman, Buck Leonard, said, "We couldn't even draw flies."[1]

To make things worse, our shining prince, Josh Gibson, the best batter in Negro League baseball, didn't live to see integration through. Heartbroken over never making it to the majors, Josh passed away shortly before Jackie's debut with the Dodgers. The Negro National League folded in 1948, and the teams that were still around went over to the Negro American League. There were still some good players in the Negro Leagues, but most of the best players—like Hank Aaron, Willie Mays, and Ernie Banks—went to the majors or the minors, or played overseas. They tried to keep the leagues going, but the best days of the Negro Leagues had long passed. The league struggled up until its last day in 1960. In all, 58 out of more than 200 Negro League players ended up in the majors.

People ask all the time if we're bitter because we weren't given the chance to play baseball in the major leagues for all of those years. Some of us are, but most of us aren't. Most Negroes back then had to work in factories,

77

wash windows, or work on some man's plantation, and they didn't get paid much for it. We were fortunate men. We got to play baseball for a living, something we would have done even if we hadn't gotten paid for it. When you can do what you love to do and get paid for it, it's a wonderful thing.

We look at guys like Bob Gibson and Ken Griffey, Jr. and smile, because we made it possible for these guys to play in the majors. If there had been no such thing as a Negro League, there would have been no Jackie Robinson or Willie Mays or Hank Aaron. These guys stand on our shoulders. We cleared the way for them and changed the course of history. And knowing that satisfies the soul. How can you be bitter about something like that?

NEGRO LEAGUERS WHO MADE IT TO THE MAJOR LEAGUES

Hank Aaron	Roy Campanella	Elston Howard	David Pope
George Altman	James "Bus" Clarkson	Monte Irvin	Curt Roberts
Sandy Amoros	Larry Doby	Sam Jethro	Jackie Robinson
Gene Baker	Lino Donoso	Connie Johnson	Antonio Hector Rodriguez
Dan Bankhead	Joe Durham	Sam Jones	Jose "Smo" Santiago
Ernie Banks	Jim Gilliam	John Irvin Kennedy	Pat Scantlebury
Frank Barnes	William "Bill" Greason	Isidoro "Izzy" Leon	Harry Simpson
Joe Black	Sam Hairston	Willie Mays	Hank Thompson
Sam Bowens	Charles "Chuck" Harmon	Minnie Minoso	Robert "Bob" Thurman
Bob Boyd	Billy Harrell	Charlie Neal	Bob Trice
Isaac "Ike" Brown	JC Hartman	Don Newcombe	Quincy Trouppe
Raymond Brown	Jehosie Heard	Ray Noble	Roberto Vargas
Willard Brown	Juan "Pancho" Herrera	Leroy "Satchel" Paige	Artie Wilson
Joe Caffie	David Hoskins	Jim Pendleton	John Wyatt

NEGRO LEAGUERS IN THE NATIONAL BASEBALL HALL OF FAME

Hank Aaron	Willie Foster	Effa Manley	Norman "Turkey" Stearnes
Ernie Banks	Andrew "Rube" Foster	Willie Mays	John "Mule" Suttles
Ray Brown	Josh Gibson	José Mendez	Ben Taylor
Willard Brown	Frank Grant	Leroy "Satchel" Paige	Cristóbal Torriente
Roy Campanella	Pete Hill	Alex Pompez	Willie Wells
Oscar Charleston	Monte Irvin	Cumberland Posey	Solomon White
Andy Cooper	William Julius "Judy" Johnson	Jackie Robinson	J.L. Wilkinson
Ray Dandridge	Buck Leonard	Wilber "Bullet Joe" Rogan	"Smokey" Joe Williams
Leon Day	John Henry "Pop" Lloyd	Louis Santop	Jud "Boojum" Wilson
Martin Dihigo	Raleigh "Biz" Mackey	Hilton Smith	

AUTHOR'S NOTE

I began my love affair with the history of the Negro Leagues while I was still a student at Pratt Institute, in 1996. I was asked to do a painting on the subject, one that I knew relatively nothing about. Around the same time that I began to do my research, Ken Burns's documentary *Baseball* was airing on PBS. I became entranced by its history and learned of baseball's overall importance, its role in the history of this country, and subsequently the world. What I found most striking was the story of the Negro Leagues, their overwhelming success despite the daunting odds against them. Their spirit of independence, having made something out of nothing at all. Armed with only their intellectual and athletic talents, and the sheer will to play the game that they loved so dearly, this group of men assumed control of their destiny. After being pushed out of the game by an overwhelming majority, African Americans, rather than giving up, formed leagues of their own, successful leagues that lasted over thirty years. Anyone who has played the game of baseball knows the feeling of batting for the first time with butterflies in your stomach, of hitting a ball squarely, being on base waiting for your teammates to bring you home, and then finally crossing home plate. The feeling of community is wonderful. And at its core, as Robert Creamer said in the Ken Burns film, "Baseball is fun." It is understandable why African Americans at that time did not want to give it up.

Although I played Little League baseball for a mere two years as a kid, those feelings and memories have lasted a lifetime. I've tried to put all of those feelings and memories of the game into the artwork for this book. I have attempted in earnest to present these men (and one woman) in all their dignity, pride, and spiritual strength. They are my heroes. They are the champions who paved the way for the great athletes who followed them: Bob Gibson, Ken Griffey, Jr., Reggie Jackson, Dave Winfield, and many, many others. Where there was no way, they made a way. I admire this independent spirit.

In keeping with this spirit, I chose to present the voice of the narrator as a collective voice, the voice of every player, the voice of we. Under the leadership of Rube Foster, who declared the leagues' independence from major league baseball by saying, "We are the ship; all else the sea," the owners and players formed and sustained a successful league, demonstrating the power of the collective. And after reading interviews and listening to former players speak about their lives in baseball, it became clear that hearing the story of Negro League baseball directly from those who experienced it firsthand made it more real, more accessible. I hope that the way I have chosen to present the story has the same effect.

The most challenging aspect of creating the artwork for the book was, without question, the research. I did find a variety of books, documentaries, and films on the subject, and a number of Web sites dedicated to preserving Negro League history. I also had a tremendous amount of help from the good folks at the Negro Leagues Baseball Museum in Kansas City and the National Baseball Hall of Fame in Cooperstown, New York, but there were some things that they, too, had not been able to conjure up. Unfortunately, much of the visual information I was looking for is lost to history—uniforms, jersey numbers, ballpark references, etc. This left me with the decision and the freedom to use a bit of artistic license to fill in the details that history has forgotten. For example, if there was a uniform color scheme I was unable to find, I would use the colors from a previous or following year (as in the Bullet Rogan portrait). If I couldn't find the color scheme for a ballpark, I would use the generic "baseball park green." Or, for example, the portrait of Cool Papa Bell shows him standing in front of the right-field wall, which is plastered with advertisements. I am fully aware that Cool Papa played center field, but the right-field wall is so visually interesting that I used a bit of license and placed him in front of it. Perhaps he was playing right field that day, or he'd just chased a fly ball to right and stopped for a photo. This may be why he appears exhausted and is bent over, resting his hands on his knees.

Despite all of its challenges, this eight-year journey from the book's beginning to completion has been a rewarding experience. It has allowed me to meet people I may not have otherwise met. I've had the opportunity to watch a baseball game and enjoy a bag of peanuts with the late great Buck O'Neil, Walt McCoy, and "Sweet Lou" Johnson. I've met baseball legends like Hank Aaron, Monte Irvin, Tony Gwynn, Dave Winfield, and Don Newcombe. I've broken bread with Spike Lee and his family, and forged friendships with the San Diego Padres and Jackie Robinson's daughter, Sharon Robinson. Some of the original paintings in this book have been exhibited in museums across the country, such as the Negro Leagues Baseball Museum and the National Baseball Hall of Fame. Most notably, I've learned so much about the Negro Leagues and American history through the first-hand accounts of former players, both in literature and spoken word. I believe I have also learned a great deal about fortitude, creativity, and excellence amid antagonism. I've learned about the strength and resilience of the human spirit, and how I can apply these principles to my life. Oprah Winfrey once said something to the effect of "How dare I be tired doing what I'm doing, knowing the trials and tribulations of my ancestors who had to work from dawn 'til dusk. They had a right to be tired. I don't." I agree.

I hope that I have done justice to these somewhat forgotten men and given them the tribute that they deserve. I have tried to honor them, to portray them as the heroes they were, and to further solidify their place in history. I hope that the reader will agree.

—K. N.

81

ACKNOWLEDGMENTS

I would like to acknowledge the following individuals and institutions who helped immensely in the creation of this book: Don Motley, Dayle Tedrow, Darcy Mitchell, Benito Hobson, Linda Barron, Marne Foster; my wife and children: Keara, Amel, and Aya Nelson; Shermaine Gary, Michael and Olivia Morris; my mother, Emily Gunter; my grandmother, Verlee Gunter-Moore; William and Valerie Ricks, Archie Taylor, and Tom Peterson; Michael Everett and the Pop Lloyd Committee; Writers House; Campos Photography; Andrea Pinkney, Garen Thomas, Jaira Placide, Brenda Bowen, Disney Book Group and Jump at the Sun/Hyperion; Phil Dixon, The National Baseball Hall of Fame, Cooperstown, New York, *Sports Illustrated*, Steve Hoffman, Bill Hill, Duane Sims, Debbie Allen, Dr. Eugene Thompson, and Dave Winfield.

Special thanks to John and Becky Moores and the San Diego Padres. This book would not have been possible without your generosity. To Steven Malk for your keen vision and encouragement. To Raymond Doswell and Bob Kendrick and the Negro Leagues Baseball Museum: thank you for your tremendous generosity and support. To Spike and Tonya Lee: for your kind and unyielding support. To Sharon Robinson for saving the day, thank you! To John McClain for your genius and motivation. A big thanks to Donna Bray and Anne Diebel: thank you for your creativity, flexibility, and professionalism. And a very special thanks to Hank Aaron, Billye Aaron, Frank Evans, Buck O'Neil, Monte Irvin, and Walter McCoy, the official consultant for the text. Thank you all for sharing your priceless memories.

BIBLIOGRAPHY

Bak, Richard. *Turkey Stearnes and the Detroit Stars: The Negro Leagues in Detroit, 1919–1933*. Detroit, Michigan: Wayne State University Press, 1994.

Holway, John. *Blackball Stars: Negro League Pioneers*. Westport, Connecticut: Meckler Books, 1988.

———. *Black Diamonds: Life in the Negro Leagues from the Men Who Lived It*. Westport, Connecticut: Meckler Books, 1989.

———. *The Complete Book of Baseball's Negro Leagues: The Other Half of Baseball History*. Winter Park, Florida: Hastings House Publishers, 2001.

———. *Josh and Satch: The Life and Times of Josh Gibson and Satchel Paige*. New York: Carroll & Graf Publishers, 1991.

———. *Voices from the Great Black Baseball Leagues*. New York: Da Capo Press, 1992.

Lester, Larry. *Black Baseball's National Showcase: The East-West All-Star Game, 1933–1953*. Lincoln, Nebraska: University of Nebraska Press, 2001.

Motley, Bob. *Ruling Over Monarchs, Giants and Stars*. Champaign, Illinois: Sports Publishing, 2007.

O'Neil, Buck. *I Was Right on Time*. New York: Fireside, 1996.

Paige, Satchel, and David Lipman. *Maybe I'll Pitch Forever*. Garden City, New York: Doubleday, 1962.

Peterson, Robert. *Only the Ball Was White: A History of Legendary Black Players and All-Black Professional Teams*. New York: Oxford University Press, 1992.

Rogosin, Donn. *Invisible Men: Life in Baseball's Negro Leagues*. New York: Atheneum Publishers, 1983.

Ward, Geoffrey C. and Burns, Ken. *Baseball: An Illustrated History*. New York: Alfred A. Knopf, 1994.

FILMOGRAPHY

There Was Always Sun Shining Someplace: Life in the Negro Baseball Leagues. Refocus Films, 1994.

Baseball: A Film by Ken Burns. PBS, 1993.

ENDNOTES

1st INNING

1. Ward/Burns, *Baseball: An Illustrated History*, p. 43

2. Holway, *Voices from the Great Black Baseball Leagues*, p. 41

3. Holway, *Blackball Stars*, p. 8

4. Burns/PBS, *Baseball*, "Shadow Ball"

5. Holway, *Blackball Stars*, p. 21

2nd INNING

1. Holway, *Voices from the Great Black Baseball Leagues*, p. 46

2. Ward/Burns, *Baseball: An Illustrated History*, p. 198

3. Peterson, *Only the Ball Was White*, Introduction

4. Holway, *Voices from the Great Black Baseball Leagues*, p. 341

5. Burns/PBS, *Baseball*, "A National Heirloom"

6. Holway, *Voices from the Great Black Baseball Leagues*, p. 222

7. Holway, *Voices from the Great Black Baseball Leagues*, p. 251

8. Holway, *Voices from the Great Black Baseball Leagues*, p. 263

3rd INNING

1. Refocus Films, *There Was Always Sun Shining Someplace: Life in the Negro Baseball Leagues*

2. Holway, *Blackball Stars*, p. 319

3. Refocus Films, *There Was Always Sun Shining Someplace: Life in the Negro Baseball Leagues*

4th INNING

1. Holway, *Blackball Stars*, p. 325

2. Burns/PBS, *Baseball*, "Shadow Ball"

5th INNING

1. Bak, *Turkey Stearnes and the Detroit Stars*, p. 11
2. Holway, *Blackball Stars*, p. 110
3. Motley, *Ruling Over Monarchs, Giants, and Stars*, p. 42
4. Holway, *Blackball Stars*, p. 353
5. Holway, *Josh and Satch*, p. 145
6. Holway, *Josh and Satch*, p. 180

6th INNING

1. Refocus Films, *There Was Always Sun Shining Someplace: Life in the Negro Baseball Leagues*
2. Refocus Films, *There Was Always Sun Shining Someplace: Life in the Negro Baseball Leagues*

7th INNING

1. Holway, *Blackball Stars*, p. 183
2. Burns/PBS, *Baseball*, "Shadow Ball"
3. Burns/PBS, Buck O'Neil interview from *Baseball*, "Shadow Ball"
4. Burns/PBS, *Baseball*, "Shadow Ball"

8th INNING

1. Burns/PBS, Buck O'Neil interview from *Baseball*, "Shadow Ball"
2. Holway, *Black Baseball Stars*, p. 324
3. Lester, *Black Baseball's National Showcase*, p. 155

9th INNING

1. Refocus Films, *There Was Always Sun Shining Someplace: Life in the Negro Baseball Leagues*
2. Ward/Burns, *Baseball: An Illustrated History*
3. Burns/PBS, *Baseball*, "Episode"
4. Holway, *Voices from the Great Black Baseball Leagues*, p. 267
5. Burns/PBS, *Baseball*, "The National Pastime"

6. Holway, *Black Diamonds*, p. 73

7. Holway, *Black Diamonds*, p. 73

8. Burns/PBS, *Baseball*, "The National Pastime"

EXTRA INNINGS

1. Holway, *Voices from the Great Black Baseball Leagues*, p. 271

INDEX

References to illustrations are in italics.